For all those who've fallen into a blank—just keep scribbling.
And to Guy, for always encouraging my scribbles.

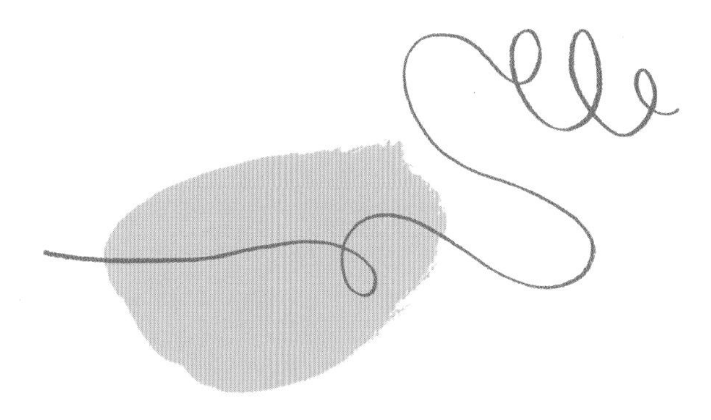

First published in 2020 by Page Street Kids
an imprint of
Page Street Publishing Co.
27 Congress Street, Suite 105
Salem, MA 01970
www.pagestreetpublishing.com

Distributed by Macmillan, sales in Canada by The Canadian Manda Group

20 21 22 23 24 CCO 5 4 3 2 1
ISBN-13: 978-1-62414-942-9 ISBN-10: 1-62414-942-1

CIP data for this book is available from the Library of Congress.

This book was typeset in Josefin Sans. The illustrations were done digitally.
Printed and bound in Shenzhen, Guangdong, China

Page Street Publishing uses only materials from suppliers
who are committed to responsible and sustainable forest management.

Page Street Publishing protects our planet by donating to nonprofits like The Trustees,
which focuses on local land conservation.

Nola's Scribbles Save the Day

CRISTINA LALLI

PAGE STREET KIDS

Nola loved her scribbles.
She took them everywhere.

They walked hand in hand down the road,
skipped together to the park, and sat side by side
at the bus stop.

With her scribbles,
Nola created her own magical world.

But when Nola tried to share
her scribbles with others,

they could never quite see what she saw.

So Nola began to hide her scribbles.
She hid with them in her own magical, lonely world.

But Nola still had a tiny hope that she could create art others would understand.

So she decided to fix her scribbles.

She bent and twisted them in ways they didn't like to bend and twist.

The harder Nola worked to change her scribbles

the harder they resisted. Still, she tried, and she tried

until her hands began to tremble

and her mind was all worn out . . .

and she drew a blank.

A **big**, boring blank.

She *fell* right into it.

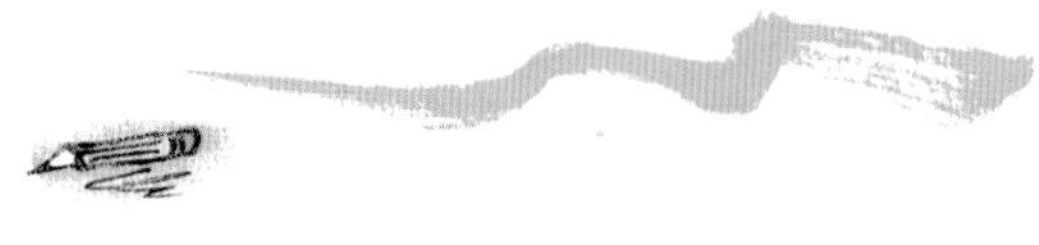

Nola blinked and stared into the nothingness.

She was stuck inside the blank and
her scribbles were nowhere to be found.

Then she heard a faint and frustrated groan.

Nola realized she wasn't alone. . . .

One by one, many others fell in too.

All types of creators were stuck
on the same blank page.

How would they get out?

Nola had an idea.

But she would have to scribble it.
What if nobody understood her scribbles?
What if the scribbles still refused to cooperate?

There was nothing left to do but try.

Nola let her scribbles be as squiggly and loopy
and zig-zaggy as ever. . . .

And it worked!

Nola and her scribbles had enthusiasm that sparked the imaginations of all the creators.

Everyone shared eagerly and built on one another's ideas.

With each inspired thought

(and very careful footing)

they created a way out—together.

Unstuck from the blank page,
Nola scribbled freely again.

She was no longer afraid to share her magical scribbles
with all her fellow creators who understood . . .
and even those who didn't.